The Elephant, the Hare and the Black Cobra

ANIMAL SHORT STORIES

Contents

PEARSON
Longman

The Underwater Elephants © Linda Newbery 2003
Brown Hare and the Fox © Martin Waddell 2003
Series editors: Martin Coles and Christine Hall

PEARSON EDUCATION LIMITED
Edinburgh Gate
Harlow
Essex CM20 2JE
England

www.longman.co.uk

The right of Rudyard Kipling, Linda Newbery and Martin Waddell to be
identified as the authors of this work has been asserted by them in accordance
with the Copyright, Designs and Patents Act, 1988.

We are grateful to A.P Watt Ltd on behalf of The National Trust for Places
of Historical Interest or Natural Beauty for permission to reproduce
Rikki-Tikki-Tavi from *The Jungle Book* by Rudyard Kipling.

First published 2003
ISBN 0582 79607 5

Illustrated by Matthew Williams (The Organisation), Merrick Durling (SGA)
and Caroline Sharpe (Heather Richards)

Printed in Great Britain by Scotprint, Haddington

The publishers' policy is to use paper manufactured from sustainable forests.

Rikki-Tikki-Tavi

by Rudyard Kipling

This is the story of the great war that Rikki-tikki-tavi fought single-handed, through the bath-rooms of the big bungalow in Segowlee cantonment. Darzee, the tailor-bird, helped him, but Rikki-tikki did the real fighting.

He was a mongoose, rather like a little cat in his fur and his tail, but quite like a weasel in his head and habits. His eyes and the end of his restless nose were pink; he could scratch himself anywhere he pleased, with any leg, front or back, that he chose to use; he could fluff up his tail till it looked like a bottle-brush, and his war-cry, as he scuttled through the long grass, was: "*Rikk-tikk-tikki-tikki-tchk!*"

One day, a high summer flood washed him out of the burrow where he lived with his father and mother, and carried him, kicking and clucking, down a roadside ditch. He found a little wisp of grass floating there, and clung to it till he lost his senses. When he revived, he was lying in the hot sun on the middle of a garden path, very draggled indeed, and a small boy was saying:

"Here's a dead mongoose. Let's have a funeral."

"No," said his mother, "let's take him in and dry him. Perhaps he isn't really dead."

They took him into the house, and a big man picked him up between his finger and thumb, and said he was not dead but half choked; so they wrapped him in cotton-wool, and warmed him and he opened his eyes and sneezed.

"Now," said the big man (he was an Englishman who had just moved into the bungalow), "don't frighten him and we'll see what he'll do."

It is the hardest thing in the world to frighten a mongoose, because he is eaten up from nose to tail with curiosity. The motto of all the mongoose family is 'Run and find out'; and Rikki-tikki was a true mongoose. He looked at the cotton-wool, decided that it was not good to eat, ran all round the table, sat up and put his fur in order, scratched himself, and jumped on the small boy's shoulder.

"Don't be frightened, Teddy," said his father. "That's his way of making friends."

"Ouch! He's tickling under my chin," said Teddy.

Rikki-tikki looked down between the boy's collar and neck, snuffed at his ear, and climbed down to the floor, where he sat rubbing his nose.

"Good gracious," said Teddy's mother, "and that's a wild creature! I suppose he's so tame because we've been kind to him."

"All mongooses are like that," said her husband. "If Teddy doesn't pick him up by the tail, or try to put him in a cage, he'll run in and out of the house all day long. Let's give him something to eat."

They gave him a little piece of raw meat. Rikki-tikki liked it immensely, and when it was finished he went out into the verandah and sat in the sunshine and fluffed up his fur to make it dry to the roots. Then he felt better.

"There are more things to find out about in this house," he said to himself, "than all my family could find out in all their lives. I shall certainly stay and find out."

He spent all that day roaming over the house. He nearly drowned himself in the bath tubs,

5

put his nose into the ink on a writing-table, and burnt it on the end of the big man's cigar, for he climbed up in the big man's lap to see how writing was done. At nightfall he ran into Teddy's nursery to watch how the kerosene-lamps were lighted, and when Teddy went to bed Rikki-tikki climbed up too; but he was a restless companion, because he had to get up and attend to every noise all through the night, and find out what made it. Teddy's mother and father came in, the last thing, to look at their boy, and Rikki-tikki was awake on the pillow.

"I don't like that," said Teddy's mother; "he may bite the child."

"He'll do no such thing," said the father. "Teddy's safer with that little beast than if he had a bloodhound to watch him. If a snake came into the nursery now –"

But Teddy's mother wouldn't think of anything so awful.

Early in the morning Rikki-tikki came to early

breakfast in the verandah riding on Teddy's shoulder, and they gave him banana and some boiled egg; and he sat on all their laps one after the other, because every well-brought-up mongoose always hopes to be a house-mongoose some day and have rooms to run about in, and Rikki-tikki's mother had told Rikki what to do if ever he came across men.

Then Rikki-tikki went out into the garden to see what was to be seen. Rikki-tikki licked his lips. "This is a splendid hunting-ground," he said, and his tail grew bottle-brushy at the thought of it, and he scuttled up and down the garden, snuffing here and there till he heard very sorrowful voices in a thorn-bush.

It was Darzee, the tailor-bird, and his wife. They had made a beautiful nest by pulling two big leaves together and stitching them up the edges with fibres, and had filled the hollow with cotton and downy fluff.

The nest swayed to and fro, as they sat on the rim and cried.

"What is the matter?" asked Rikki-tikki.

"We are very miserable," said Darzee. "One of our babies fell out of the nest yesterday, and Nag ate him."

"H'm!" said Rikki-tikki, "that is very sad – but I am a stranger here. Who is Nag?"

Darzee and his wife only cowered down in the nest without answering, for from the thick grass at the foot of the bush there came a low hiss – a horrid cold sound that made Rikki-tikki jump back two clear feet. Then inch by inch out of the grass rose up the head and spread hood of Nag, the big black cobra, and he was five feet long from tongue to tail. When he had lifted one-third of himself clear of the ground, he stayed balancing to and fro exactly as a dandelion-tuft balances in the wind, and he looked at Rikki-tikki with the wicked snake's eyes that never change their expression, whatever the snake may be thinking of.

"Who is Nag?" said he. "*I* am Nag. The great god Brahm put his mark upon all our people when the first cobra spread his hood to keep the sun off Brahm as he slept. Look, and be afraid!"

He spread out his hood more than ever, and Rikki-tikki saw the spectacle-mark on the back of it that looks exactly like the eye part of a hook-and-eye fastening. He was afraid for the minute; but it is impossible for a mongoose to stay frightened for any length of time, and though Rikki-tikki had never met a live cobra before, his mother had fed him on dead ones, and he knew that all a grown mongoose's business in life was to fight and eat snakes. Nag knew that too, and at the bottom of his cold heart he was afraid.

"Well," said Rikki-tikki, and his tail began to fluff up again, "marks or no marks, do you think it is right for you to eat fledglings out of a nest?"

Nag was thinking to himself, and watching the least little movement in the grass behind Rikki-tikki. He knew that mongooses in the garden meant death sooner or later for him and his family, but he wanted to get Rikki-tikki off his guard. So he dropped his head a little, and put it on one side.

"Let us talk," he said. "You eat eggs. Why should not I eat birds?"

"Behind you! Look behind you!" sang Darzee.

Rikki-tikki knew better than to waste time in

fledglings: young birds

staring. He jumped up in the air as high as he could go, and just under him whizzed by the head of Nagaina, Nag's wicked wife. She had crept up behind him as he was talking, to make an end of him; and he heard her savage hiss as the stroke missed. He came down almost across her back, and if he had been an old mongoose he would have known that then was the time to break her back with one bite; but he was afraid of the terrible lashing return-stroke of the cobra. He bit, indeed, but did not bite long enough, and he jumped clear of the whisking tail, leaving Nagaina torn and angry.

"Wicked, wicked Darzee!" said Nag, lashing up as high as he could reach toward the nest in the thorn-bush; but Darzee had built it out of reach of snakes, and it only swayed to and fro.

Rikki-tikki felt his eyes growing red and hot (when a mongoose's eyes grow red, he is angry), and he sat back on his tail and hind legs like a little kangaroo, and looked all round him, and chattered with rage. But Nag and Nagaina had disappeared into the grass. When a snake misses its stroke, it never says anything or gives any sign of what it means to do next. Rikki-tikki did not care to follow them, for he did not feel sure that he could manage two snakes at once. So he trotted off to the gravel path near the house, and sat down to think. It was a serious matter for him.

If you read the old books of natural history, you will find they say that when the mongoose fights the snake and happens to get bitten, he runs off and eats some herb that cures him. That is not true. The victory is only a matter of quickness of eye and quickness of foot – snake's blow against mongoose's jump – and as no eye can follow the motion of a snake's head when it strikes, that makes things much more wonderful than any magic herb. Rikki-tikki knew he was a young mongoose, and it made him all the more pleased to think that he had managed to escape a blow from behind. It gave him confidence in himself, and when Teddy came running down the path, Rikki-tikki was ready to be petted.

But just as Teddy was stooping, something flinched a little in the dust, and a tiny voice said:

"Be careful.
I am death!" It was
Karait, the dusty
brown snakeling that lies for
choice on the dusty earth; and
his bite is as dangerous as the
cobra's. But he is so small that nobody thinks of
him, and so he does the more harm to people.

Rikki-tikki's eyes grew red again, and he
danced up to Karait with the peculiar rocking,
swaying motion that he had inherited from his
family. It looks very funny, but it is so perfectly
balanced a gait that you can fly off from it at any
angle you please; and in dealing with snakes this
is an advantage. If Rikki-tikki had only known, he
was doing a much more dangerous thing than
fighting Nag, for Karait is so small, and can turn
so quickly, that unless Rikki bit him close to the
back of the head, he would get the return-stroke
in his eye or lip. But Rikki did not know: his eyes
were all red, and he rocked back and forth,
looking for a good place to hold. Karait struck
out. Rikki jumped sideways and tried to run in,
but the wicked little dusty gray head lashed within
a fraction of his shoulder, and he had to jump over
the body, and the head followed his heels close.

Teddy shouted to the house: "Oh, look here!

gait: a way of walking

Our mongoose is killing a snake"; and Rikki-tikki heard a scream from Teddy's mother. His father ran out with a stick, but by the time he came up, Karait had lunged out once too far, and Rikki-tikki had sprung, jumped on the snake's back, dropped his head far between his fore-legs, bitten as high up the back as he could get hold, and rolled away. That bite paralysed Karait, and Rikki-tikki was just going to eat him up from the tail, after the custom of his family at dinner, when he remembered that a full meal makes a slow mongoose, and if he wanted all his strength and quickness ready, he must keep himself thin.

He went away for a dust-bath under the castor-oil bushes, while Teddy's father beat the dead Karait. "What is the use of that?" thought Rikki-tikki. "I have settled it all"; and then Teddy's mother picked him up from the dust and hugged him, crying that he had saved Teddy from death, and Teddy's father said that he was a providence, and Teddy looked on with big scared eyes. Rikki-tikki was rather amused at all the fuss, which, of course, he did not understand. Teddy's mother might just as well have petted Teddy for playing in the dust. Rikki was thoroughly enjoying himself.

That night, at dinner, walking to and fro

providence: a protector/carer provided by nature

among the wine-glasses on the table, he could have stuffed himself three times over with nice things; but he remembered Nag and Nagaina, and though it was very pleasant to be patted and petted by Teddy's mother, and to sit on Teddy's shoulder, his eyes would get red from time to time, and he would go off into his long war-cry of '*Rikk-tikk-tikki-tikki-tchk!*'

Teddy carried him off to bed, and insisted on Rikki-tikki sleeping under his chin. Rikki-tikki was too well bred to bite or scratch, but as soon as Teddy was asleep he went off for his nightly walk round the house.

Rikki-tikki listened. The house was as still as still, but he thought he could just catch the faintest '*scratch-scratch*' in the world – a noise as faint as that of a wasp walking on a window-pane – the dry scratch of a snake's scales on brickwork.

"That's Nag or Nagaina," he said to himself; "and he's crawling into the bath-room sluice."

He stole off to Teddy's bath-room, and he heard Nag and Nagaina whispering together outside in the moonlight.

sluice: a drain that can be opened to control the water flow

"When the house is emptied of people," said Nagaina to her husband, "*he* will have to go away, and then the garden will be our own again. Go in quietly, and remember that the big man who killed Karait is the first one to bite. Then come out and tell me, and we will hunt for Rikki-tikki together."

"But are you sure that there is anything to be gained by killing the people?" said Nag.

"Everything. When there were no people in the bungalow, did we have any mongoose in the garden? So long as the bungalow is empty, we are king and queen of the garden; and remember that as soon as our eggs in the melon-bed hatch, our children will need room and quiet."

"I had not thought of that," said Nag. "I will go, but there is no need that we should hunt for Rikki-tikki afterward. I will kill the big man and his wife, and the child if I can, and come away quietly. Then the bungalow will be empty, and Rikki-tikki will go."

Rikki-tikki tingled all over with rage and hatred at this, and then Nag's head came through the sluice, and his five feet of cold body followed it.

Angry as he was, Rikki-tikki was very frightened as he saw the size of the big cobra. Nag coiled himself down, coil by coil, round the bulge at the bottom of the water-jar, and Rikki-tikki stayed still as death. After an hour he began to move, muscle by muscle, toward the jar. Nag was asleep, and Rikki-tikki looked at his big back, wondering which would be the best place for a good hold. "If I don't break his back at the first jump," said Rikki, "he can still fight; and if he fights – O Rikki!" He looked at the thickness of the neck below the hood, but that was too much for him; and a bite near the tail would only make Nag savage.

"It must be the head," he said at last; "the head above the hood; and when I am once there, I must not let go."

Then he jumped. The head was lying a little

clear of the water-jar, under the curve of it; and, as his teeth met, Rikki braced his back against the bulge of the red earthenware to hold down the head. This gave him just one second's purchase, and he made the most of it. Then he was battered to and fro as a rat is shaken by a dog – to and fro on the floor, up and down, and round in great circles; but his eyes were red, and he held on as the body cart-whipped over the floor, upsetting the tin dipper and the soap-dish and the flesh-brush, and banged against the tin side of the bath. As he held he closed his jaws tighter and tighter, for he was sure he would be banged to death, and, for the honour of his family, he preferred to be found with his teeth locked. He was dizzy, aching, and felt shaken to pieces when something went off like a thunderclap just behind him; a hot wind knocked him senseless, and red fire singed his fur. The big man had been wakened by the noise, and had fired both barrels of a shotgun into Nag just behind the hood.

Rikki-tikki held on with his eyes shut, for now he was quite sure he was dead; but the head did not move, and the big man picked him up and said: "It's the mongoose again, Alice; the little chap has saved our lives now." Then Teddy's mother came in with a very white face, and saw what was left of Nag, and Rikki-tikki dragged himself to Teddy's bedroom and spent half the rest of the night shaking himself tenderly to find out whether he really was broken into forty pieces, as he fancied.

When morning came he was very stiff, but well pleased with his doings.

Without waiting for breakfast, Rikki-tikki ran to the thorn-bush where Darzee was singing a song of triumph at the top of his voice. The news of Nag's death was all over the garden, for the sweeper had thrown the body on the rubbish-heap.

"Nag is dead – is dead – is dead!" sang Darzee. "The valiant Rikki-tikki caught him by the head and held fast. The big man brought the bang-stick, and Nag fell in two pieces! He will never eat my babies again."

The Underwater Elephants
by Linda Newbery

You've probably wondered why elephants have
such long noses.

Have they always had them?

Don't they get in the way?

If trunks are such a good idea, why don't all
animals have them? Why don't *we* have them?

The answer is simple. Elephants' trunks are
breathing tubes, like snorkels. Long ago, when
rivers were deep and wide, and forests covered
most of the world, elephants lived underwater.

Not many people know that. But you do.

* * * * *

When Mango was a baby, she and her family
lived in a deep, fast-flowing river. While the sun
baked the land all through the long summer days,
the elephant family stayed in the water, with just
the tips of their trunks showing on the rippled

surface. If you walked along the riverbank – but no-one ever did – all you'd see would be the very tips of eleven elephant trunks, from Gumbo's, the biggest, down to Mango's, the smallest. You wouldn't have known what they were. You'd have thought, "What are those? Strange water plants? Weird fish?"

The older elephants could stay like that for hours, quite still. When they got hungry, they'd reach up to the riverbank and snatch a mouthful of sweet grass or juicy rushes. If you saw *that*, you'd jump back from the water's edge and stay well clear. "Snakes!" you'd think. "I must be more careful where I put my feet, or they'll pull me in!"

For Mango and her cousin Rollo, the river was a marvellous adventure playground. As long as they raised their trunks to the surface every few minutes, they could play chase, and hide-and-seek in the weeds, and loop-the-loop.

(What stroke did they swim? Ellie-paddle!)

When they got tired, they could hang below the surface with the grown-ups, enjoying the cool flow of water and the brush of fish against their soft skin. (Oh, yes. Elephants had soft skin, then. It was only later, when they had to leave the water, that their skins got tough and cracked and leathery.)

Mango's favourite resting position was upside-down, with all four feet flat on the surface. She daydreamed as she floated, gazing up at the ripply sky where birds flew like fish and the sun was a giant yellow lily.

Sometimes a frog mistook one of Mango's feet for a lily pad, and sat on it. That tickled, and made her giggle and splutter and turn right way up.

The elephants would have stayed in their underwater world forever – swimming, eating, playing. They rarely came out, except to enjoy a rain shower.

But then two things happened. The first was that the weather got hotter and hotter and the river got shallower.

And the second thing was crocodiles.

* * * * *

At first, crocodiles weren't much bother. There weren't many and they weren't very big. If an elephant and a crocodile met in the water, they were polite to each other. The river was so big and wide that there was plenty of room for everyone.

But the warm water and the food must have suited the crocodiles. Each brood of babies grew bigger than its parents, with longer and sharper teeth, and hungrier appetites. And the more crocodiles there were, the bossier they became. You'd have thought they owned the river.

Billow, Mango's mother, showed her how to see off a small crocodile. With the tip of her trunk she tickled its soft tummy. An elephant's trunk is the perfect tickler! Soon the croc was laughing so much that it had to crawl out of the river to rest on the bank.

(If you came along *then*, you'd decide to be somewhere else. Because it's impossible to tell a laughing crocodile from one that's flashing all its teeth at you.)

But there was one half-grown crocodile called Sneaker who couldn't be tickled. He liked to sneak up on the elephants from behind. His favourite trick was to grab Mango's tail in his jaws and hang on to it, no matter how fast she swam away or how hard she wriggled. It began as a game, but when a young elephant called Wallow was dozing alone in the river, Sneaker sneaked up behind and bit off his tail altogether. Snap! And poor Wallow, feeling silly and ashamed and sore, was left with a stump. The croc swam away, grinning, with the end of Wallow's tail dangling from his teeth.

Wallow hoped his tail would grow back. Mango kept looking, hoping she could say it had grown just a bit, but it never did.

Mango managed to keep her tail, though she had a few scars, each with a memory of a painful nip. But it was hard to relax in the river when any green floating thing (however hard it pretended to be a log) could suddenly open its jaws and reveal rows of sharp, shining teeth. Sneaker had acted very sneakily, Mango thought. Games were all very well – chewing off tails just wasn't fair!

But it was no use trying to explain fairness to Sneaker. He'd give one of his slitty sideways looks and glide into the river without even a splash.

Soon, Mango had a chance to get her own back. *Two* chances.

Even a crocodile has to sleep sometimes, and when she saw Sneaker curled up on the riverbank she couldn't resist tiptoeing close to him.

"Never trust a crocodile," Billow had told her. "They often *pretend* to be asleep."

Mango felt sure Sneaker wasn't pretending. Carefully, she extended her trunk. She took a deep

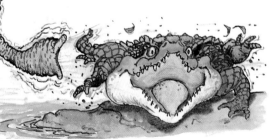

breath and trumpeted into his ear with all her might.

Sneaker was so startled, he nearly tied himself in a knot! When he came to his senses and saw it was only Mango, he glared at her and slithered away in the water with a menacing snap of his teeth.

Two days later, Mango did something even more unwise. While Rollo and Wallow were playing loop-the-loop, she swam off alone. She paddled downstream, far from the herd.

This was risky, she knew. 'NEVER go farther away than trumpeting distance' – that was the rule. You never knew who you might meet.

But the water was cool and silky, and the weed was green and wavy, and every time Mango reached a bend, she thought, "Just a little bit farther."

And –

"Just a very little bit farther …"

And –

"Just a little way round the next bend, just far enough to see …"

And what she saw was Sneaker.

Mango raised her head above water. Sneaker had found a new place to sleep, in wet, oozy mud. His tail was curled round his back feet and he was snoring gently.

She waded into the shallows, watching carefully in case one slitty eye should open. But no. Sneaker was heavily asleep, snoring peacefully.

"Do I dare?" Mango thought.

Yes, she did.

In fact she couldn't resist!

She lurched ashore and grabbed Sneaker's tail with her trunk. Then she tugged as hard as she could.

Sneaker woke with a snort. His eyes opened,

narrowed and glared. His jaws gaped. His teeth snapped. He snapped at the air, not at Mango, who ran backwards very fast, still pulling round and round in mad circles.

When she was so dizzy that she hardly knew which way was up, she stopped and let go. Sneaker gave a groggy glare, hissed loudly and slithered into his hole.

Mango had frightened herself. She'd better swim back to the others as fast as she could, and pretend nothing had happened.

Sploshing into the river, she saw a grey domed head, two sad eyes and two ears that flapped in the current. It was Sorrow, her great-aunt.

"Mango, that was very silly," Sorrow chided. "We've only got one river and we have to share it with the crocs. They're not the best neighbours, but we mustn't annoy them. You've made Sneaker angry, and that's bad news for all of us. Elephants never forget – but neither do crocodiles."

* * * * *

Sorrow was right. It was open warfare now.
Once, Sneaker had been playful – now he was
downright nasty.

The elephants worried about their trunks, so
tempting for a sharp-toothed crocodile in search
of revenge. One snap – and there would be a very
ashamed elephant with no trunk! Losing a tail
was bad enough. Losing a trunk would make life
very difficult indeed. You couldn't really call
yourself an elephant, with your trunk missing.

Mango felt guilty and tried to behave very well
for the next few days. "It's all my fault," she
whispered to her friend, Rollo.

Sneaker summoned all his friends and relations.
Now, crocodiles log-jammed the river in both
directions. There were so many that the river
seemed to bristle with teeth.

Gumbo made an announcement – the older
elephants would take turns on guard duty. One
upstream, one downstream, at each end of the
family group. Even the biggest, fiercest crocodile

wouldn't dare approach a big elephant; an elephant's tusks could throw a croc right out of the water. Gumbo's plan meant that everyone not on duty could play, sleep or float without worrying about snapping teeth.

The other problem was harder to solve.

Each year it rained less than the last, and the river got shallower and shallower. The new babies were small enough to swim, but Mango was bigger now. She and Rollo couldn't find water deeper than their shoulders. They stood with the others, hot and disappointed, while their skins toughened in the baking sun. They stamped at the water and sprayed themselves using their trunks. It wasn't the same as floating, deep and cool. Sometimes they'd lie down and roll, just to get themselves wet all over.

Gumbo heaved himself to his feet, and water poured off him. In moments his skin changed from glossy underwater grey to dull, sun-dried mud colour.

There must be another river! A deeper river. Mango stared across the plain, across miles and miles of bleached grass, to the distant forest trees.

"Come on," she whispered to Rollo, when the others settled for their afternoon doze. "Let's explore."

Mango and Rollo walked slowly through the long grass of the plain. The sun beat down and they flapped their ears to keep cool. Sharp stalks prickled their feet and insects buzzed around their heads. Mango didn't like it, but she could see the forest and the shade of trees like a dark pool of water.

Three antelopes bounded up and sprang across the grass. Mango tried to copy them, but she was too heavy and could only gallumph. Rollo trumpeted with laughter, then stopped in mid-hoot, pointing his trunk at two tall, graceful creatures with enormously long necks. They were walking in their long-legged lollopy way towards the forest edge.

"Giraffes," Mango whispered. Billow had told her about them.

When the giraffes reached the trees, they began to nibble the highest leaves. Their necks were so long that their heads showed through the branches. Their gentle eyes gazed down at the two elephants.

"Leaves!" Rollo said. "I wonder what they taste like?"

Mango stretched up and grasped a trunkful. She put them into her mouth. She chewed thoughtfully and swallowed. Delicious! She reached for more.

* * * * *

Very nervously, Mango and Rollo approached Gumbo with their idea. Gumbo, by far the biggest elephant, could be short-tempered. His watery eyes stared.

"That," he said, "is a preposterous idea, children. A nonsensical, ridiculous, preposterous idea. Go away and eat grass." His trunk curled up in a sneer.

Mango and Rollo turned away, ears drooping.

Wise old Sorrow had overheard. "It *is* a good idea," she whispered, "but you know what Gumbo's like. Much too proud to listen. You'll have to make him think he thought of it himself."

Mango and Rollo looked at each other.

Then Mango started planning.

* * * * *

They waited till Gumbo was asleep, slumped in a trickle of river. Gumbo asleep was an alarming

sight. His mud-grey sides were a shuddering
mountain. His snores were a rumbling thunder.
The hiss of his breath was a snake chorus.

Mango and Rollo crept close, hardly daring to
breathe.

With her trunk, Mango carried a big branch
of acacia leaves. She and Rollo had walked
all the way back to the forest to fetch it.

She held it close to Gumbo's head. She shook it gently so that the leaves rustled, sounding like cool rain.

Rollo made the bird call he had practised – a soft, flutey call, like the trickle of a shallow stream.

Mango let the acacia leaves touch Gumbo's hide, like dappled water. "Trees, *trees*," she whispered in his ear. "Elephants need trees."

Gumbo's ear flapped. The tip of his trunk twitched. He curled his trunk to pull off a few acacia leaves, and he chewed them very thoughtfully, still fast asleep.

He slept for two more hours. When he stirred Mango and Rollo moved away, respectfully. Gumbo planted his front feet in the water, then heaved, lurched and stood upright. Water gushed from his legs and tail. He looked round at the herd. Then he raised his trunk and trumpeted – so loudly that all the nearby birds rose in a cloud and flapped away.

"I have made a decision," he announced grandly.

All the elephants gathered.

"Since we can't live underwater," Gumbo told them, "we'll live under trees. The cool shade will be like water. There is plentiful food. We will use our trunks to pluck leaves. There will be new, delicious flavours to explore. We'll find forest streams and swamps. It will be the next best thing to living underwater. And," he added with a fierce glance down the river, "there will be *no crocodiles.*"

A floating log twitched and showed its teeth. It smiled nastily. Wallow gave a shudder and moved closer to the herd.

"We'll leave straight away," Gumbo said, "now that my mind's made up."

All the elephants flapped their ears, which is an elephant's way of clapping.

"What a brilliant idea!" said wise old Sorrow.

Gumbo smiled modestly. "It came to me in a dream," he said. "Just like that."

* * * * *

The elephants moved across the plain, following Gumbo. One by one, they disappeared into the deep shade of the forest.

Mango turned and lifted her trunk to trumpet a

goodbye to Sneaker. "Bet you wish you were coming!" she yelled.

The crocodile watched sadly from the riverbank. He would miss them.

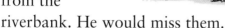

* * * * *

Mango is a wise old elephant now. She has children and grandchildren of her own.

They walk from forest to forest, looking for deep shade and delicious things to eat. They find cool grass to lie on and swamps to wallow in. Birdsong at dawn sounds more sweetly to an elephant than the snapping of crocodiles' teeth.

But an elephant never forgets, and one of the things an elephant never forgets is where it came from.

If ever you see a sleeping elephant, watch it very carefully. Slowly, it will smile. Its feet will start to paddle. Its trunk will stretch upwards, remembering that it was once a breathing tube.

Then you will know that your elephant is back in the past. It is dreaming of those happy, floating, paddling, wallowing, loop-the-loop days, when elephants lived underwater.

Brown Hare and the Fox
by Martin Waddell

Nora came every year to stay with Grannie
Brennan, in the old stone house by Banagher
Lake.

"I want to go, too," her brother Donal insisted.

"You're not old enough," said his Mammy.

"I am so," said Donal. "I'm nearly six."

That's how Nora wound up looking after one
very small brother, which didn't please her one bit.

"Don't let him annoy Grannie Brennan,"
Mammy told Nora.

"You're to do what I say!" Nora told Donal.

"Well, maybe I might," grinned small Donal.

Grannie's house was along a stone lane that led
to the shore of Banagher Lake. Granda's fields ran
from the shore of the lake, up to the plantation
trees that grew on the low slopes of Croopey
Mountain. Grannie didn't farm Granda's fields
anymore now Granda was dead. The fields were

35

farmed by her neighbour, Jack Rooney.

It was not at all like the city they came from. There were only two houses, Grannie Brennan's and Jack Rooney's, along the steep side of the mountain. No streets and no cars, and no parks and no shops.

The grocery van came twice a week down Grannie Brennan's lane, and that's where Grannie Brennan did her shopping. Jack Rooney came over the fields every day to see Grannie, and he bought the rest of the stuff that she needed from town.

"A shop in a van?" Donal asked Nora. "Will there be sweets in the van?"

"There'll be sweets," Nora told him.

That pleased Donal, but ...

"Has Grannie Brennan got a TV?" Donal asked anxiously.

"There's not much time for TV at Grannie Brennan's house," Nora said.

That didn't please Donal, but he thought he could play with his electronic games.

"I'll take you to see old Brown Hare," Nora said, trying to cheer Donal up. "She lives over in Jack Rooney's fields. I saw her the last time I was there."

"What's a hare?" Donal asked.

"You'll see," Nora said. "It's a bit like a very big rabbit."

"I want to see old Brown Hare," Donal told Grannie Brennan that night, as they sat by the fire in her house.

"You'd have to go out in the cold fields at dawn to see her," Grannie said.

"I don't mind that one bit," Donal said ... but he *did* mind, next morning.

"If you want to see old Brown Hare, then you have to get up!" Nora told him, and she got him up from his bed.

They had cups of tea in the kitchen, and then they put on their coats and their boots and went out of the house. They trudged up the side of Great Granda's stone-wall-that-was-built-clearing-the-field-years-ago. They went up Granda's fields to the plantation trees, and then they walked by the edge of the trees, to the field above Jack Rooney's house.

37

Jack's curtains were closed. Nothing stirred round his house.

"That wise man is still in his bed!" grumbled Grannie, who had to stop to draw breath.

"He won't see Brown Hare like me!" Donal said, sounding pleased with himself.

"He's seen Brown Hare before, many a time," Nora said. "Brown Hare lives here. Brown Hare is Jack Rooney's hare."

"Hares belong to no man," Grannie said. "The way a hare thinks, she belongs to herself, and the fields belong to her."

"You'd best not say that to Jack Rooney," said Nora. "He says all these fields are his, not Brown Hare's."

"Does Jack Rooney not like Brown Hare?" Donal asked Grannie.

"She eats the crop from the fields," Grannie said. "Jack Rooney farms for a living. Why should he like old Brown Hare?"

They stopped by the black rock, where they could look down over the roof of Jack Rooney's house at the low fields by the lake.

"Keep very still," Nora told Donal. "Don't move at all. Brown Hare has her young ones hidden down there in nests she made for them in the fields. If she thinks we are here, she won't show herself."

"Like birds' nests?" said Donal. "Like birds' nests with eggs?"

"They're not eggs," Nora told him. "They are little animals. They're hidden away in places she makes in the grass, or close by the sides of big stones where they can't be seen. They each have a place of their own, so she won't lose them all if a fox comes and finds one."

"Like burrows and rabbits?" said Donal.

"Not burrows," said Nora. "Just places on top of the ground, or in small dips in the field, or maybe somewhere in the reeds round the lake."

"I think that is silly," said Donal. "Rabbits in burrows are best."

"Keep quiet," Grannie told him. "You'll scare old Brown Hare."

A cold morning mist hung over the lake.

"I'm bored," Donal said, shifting about. "Can I go climbing the rock?"

"No you cannot!" Nora hissed.

"But …"

"Hold your wheest!" said old Grannie.

"What's a wheest?" Donal whispered.

"She means, 'Shut up', Donal!" Nora told him. "It's just one of Grannie's old words."

"Stay still, and wait for Brown Hare to show

up," Grannie said. "Brown Hare's what we've come out to see."

Donal stayed still. His fingers were cold and so were his feet. His boots were too big. They were an old pair of Grannie's he'd borrowed, because he didn't want to spoil his new trainers in the wet grass.

"Look at me breathing smoke like a dragon," Donal whispered.

"Wheest!" Grannie said.

Then Nora saw something move.

She nudged Grannie and pointed down to the end of Jack Rooney's cow field, the one with the reeds by the lake. There were no cows in the field that morning. Jack Rooney had moved them four fields away, to fresh grass.

"Something moved!" Nora whispered to Grannie.

It was Brown Hare.

Brown Hare rose from the hollow in the field, where she'd been hidden. They could see her long back and big ears. She stood stiff backed, with her ears up.

Then she wizzled and twizzled and wrinkled her nose, and she sniffed at the air, and then ...

"There goes Brown Hare!" Nora told Donal.

Hoppity-hoppity-hoppity-hop.

Brown Hare stopped.

She wizzled and twizzled and wrinkled her nose, looking round at the field.

"Is that it?" Donal whispered. "Is that all she does?"

"Be quiet!" Nora whispered. "Hares have sharp ears. She can hear a twig snap four fields away."

Hoppity-hoppity-hoppity-hop.

Brown Hare disappeared into a dip in the field, by the bright yellow gorse, and was gone where they couldn't see her.

"Can we go home for our breakfast?" Donal asked, hopefully.

"One of her young ones must be hidden in there," Nora said. "We're staying here till she comes out again."

Donal had lost interest. He was cold and fed up, and his feet were like ice inside the too-big boots. They stood for what seemed a long time to Donal, but there was no sign of Brown Hare.

"Where is she, Grannie?" asked Nora.

"She's maybe followed the dip and come out in the next field," said Grannie. "If she did we can't see her from here."

"Can we go where we can see her?" asked
Nora.

"I want to go home," muttered Donal.

"You're just a nuisance, our Donal,"
said Nora.

Grannie Brennan and Nora went
into the trees above the next field.
Donal came trailing behind them
in his too-big boots.

Grannie showed them where to stand so that
Brown Hare wouldn't see them. And then ...

"Look Nora! Look Donal!" said Grannie.
"Look over there by the edge of the gorse, two
fields away, over there."

Nora looked. At first she saw nothing at all ...
then she saw something move, as it slinked
through the rocks and the gorse at the edge of the
field.

"What is it?" asked Nora.

"It's a fox," Grannie said.

"Oh lovely," said Nora. "Isn't he glowy red! He's just gorgeous … look Donal."

But Donal was too cold to be bothered looking.

"What's he doing?" asked Nora.

"He'll be searching for Brown Hare's young ones in their hidden places," said Grannie. "He's wanting his breakfast like our Donal is. Donal's breakfast is toast. The fox's breakfast could be our Brown Hare."

"Do foxes eat hares?" Donal said, suddenly interested again, despite the cold.

"Foxes eat any mortal thing they can lay hold of," Grannie said. "I'd better be telling Jack Rooney this one is about, so he can mind his chickens."

Nora had gone pale.

The fox was slinking along the line of the gorse, in and out, in and out … now they could see him, now they couldn't. Then …

"Look. Over there!" Nora whispered.

Over there was Brown Hare, two fields away from the fox.

Brown Hare was standing very still, head up in the air. She sniffed at the air.

"She smells fox … but she doesn't know where the fox is," Grannie whispered.

"Run!" Nora said. "Why doesn't she run away?"

"She fears for her young ones," said Grannie. "Watch this now. You'll see what she does. She'll lead him away from her young ones."

Red Fox came over the old tumbled stone wall, one field away from Brown Hare.

Brown Hare stood upright, with her long ears in the air and her nose twitching.

The fox disappeared in the long grass by the stones, making straight for Brown Hare.

"He knows she is there," whispered Grannie.

"He can't see her," said Donal. "How does the fox know where she is?"

"He has her scent," Grannie said softly. "Look now … watch Brown Hare."

Brown Hare wizzled and twizzled and wrinkled her nose, and wizzled and twizzled again, and then …

… she was off.

Hoppity-hoppity-hoppity-hop.

Brown Hare was off, and so was the fox.

Brown Hare twisted and turned as she ran. The fox twisted and turned after Brown Hare.

They ran through one field, and another. Brown Hare turned by the gorse and cut back. Then she stopped by the stone wall between the two fields.

The fox had stopped, too.

"He's lost her," said Donal.

Then the fox moved again, and so did Brown Hare.

She was over the tumbled stone wall, and along the line of the wall, then she turned back and ran over the field, as the fox leaped on top of the wall.

Donal saw the flash of his tail, and the twist of his head as he looked, and then he was after Brown Hare again.

They ran
and they ran
and they ran
and they ran twisting
this way and *this way*
and *this way* and *that*.

Every turn Brown Hare took, the fox followed.

Brown Hare turned past the rocks and the heather beyond Jack Rooney's barn, along the hedge, through the brambles and thorns.

"They're in our fields now," Grannie told Nora.

"Keep running Brown Hare!" Nora called.

The fox and Brown Hare sped over the fields. Brown Hare turned again and again and again,

this way and *this way*

and *this way* and *that*,

that way and *that way*

and *that way* and *this*

heading back up the fields toward the woods.

"She's coming this way!" Nora shouted.

Brown Hare went by them and into the trees, with the red fox running fast behind her.

The last thing Nora saw was the flash of his tail, as he disappeared in the thicket among the tall trees.

"Will he catch her?" asked Nora.

"Will he eat her?" said Donal, looking at Grannie.

"I don't know!" Grannie said. "But that old hare of yours knows her way through the trees. She has a pile of hare tricks … and the fox was a good way behind her. She let him see her … then she led him away from the places where her young ones were hid. She'll lose the old fox, and then she'll come back to care for her babies."

"*If* the fox doesn't catch her," said Nora.

"How will we know?" asked Donal.

"Well … we'll put our coats on tonight and come out. We'll watch over the field where her young ones are hidden. If Brown Hare is all right, she will come back and take them somewhere else, where they'll maybe be safe from the fox," Grannie said.

"What if Brown Hare doesn't come?" Nora said.

"Then we'll have cold feet for nothing," said Grannie.

They waited all day, and just after sunset they went out to the fields, wrapped up in their coats and their boots.

And …

The fields were cold and empty. There was no sign of Brown Hare.

The moon rose, and still they waited. Nothing stirred in the fields below them, nothing moved in the shadows.

The moonlight spread slowly. It made a shiny path over the lake, from one side to the other.

The only sound was the soft lap of the water amongst the reeds.

"Brown Hare must be dead," Donal said. He'd gone pale, and his small face was peaky. "The old fox has ate her."

Nora said nothing. There were tears in her eyes. She had her heart in her mouth. She didn't want Brown Hare to be dead.

Then …

"Look there!" Grannie whispered.

It was Brown Hare in the field with the reeds by the lake.

She wizzled and twizzled and wrinkled her nose, and then she slipped away into the reeds.

"It's all right!" Donal said, hugging Grannie.

Nora just stood there and beamed. She'd no need for tears now.

Brown Hare had escaped from the fox.